AF584807

First published in 2023 by

wdog.com.au
Melbourne, Australia

A catalogue record for this book is available from the National Library of Australia

ISBN: 9781742036731 (hbk)

Printed and bound by Everbest Ltd.

10 9 8 7 6 5 4 3 2 1   23 24 25 26 27 28

FSC® is a non-profit international organisation established to promote the responsible management of the world's forests.

Walking the same track filling our footprints with knowledge for a better future while remembering the past pain of my people.

D.S.

To my clever and creative mum, Pam, who supports everything I do.

N.G.

This is an invitation to healing
and walking together proper way –
One heart One people One mob.

J.C.

Thank you to the photographers of these stunning artworks; René Bahloo, Mike Korsos, Amy Ocean and Jordi Goya.

Aboriginal and Torres Strait Island Peoples are warned that this book contains an image of a person who has died.

DUNCAN SMITH & NICOLE GODWIN

with paintings by JANDAMARRA CADD

Listen.

And you will hear
the voices of Ancestors.

Speaking to us.

Guiding us.

Listen carefully to the voices of First Peoples.

Seeking respect.

Laying bare the deep scars of the past through truth-telling.

Leading us to healing.

Listen deeply
to Elders.

Speaking
the first languages
of Country.

Telling Dreaming stories that fill our hearts.

Talking about what Treaty means.

Sharing Songlines.

Generously leading us
on the path to knowledge
of culture,
of Country.

To understand.
To reconcile.

Listen with openness.

To Voices of the past
and present, telling
their stories.

Guiding us.

Walking together in the footprints of Ancestors.

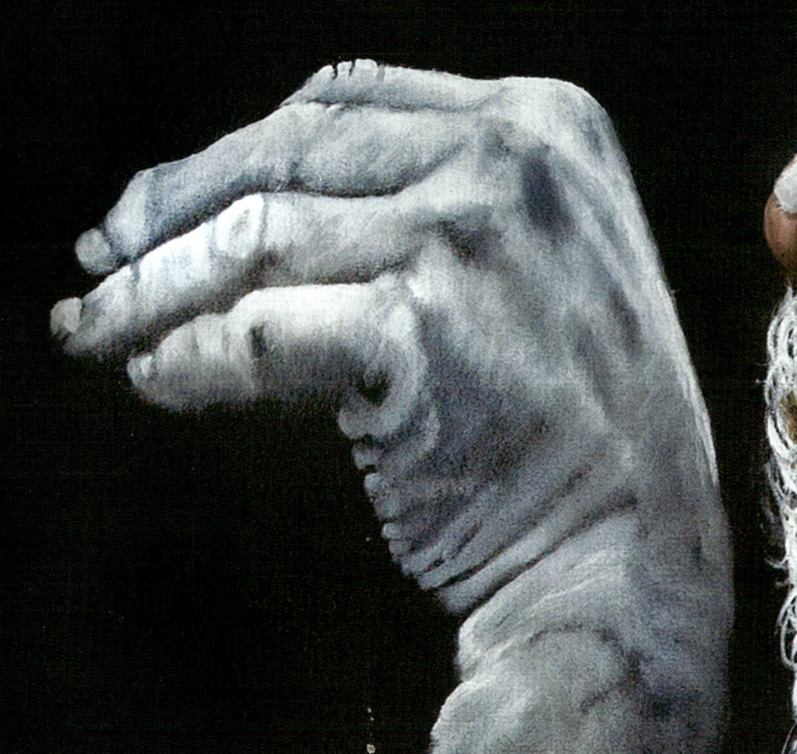

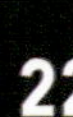

JANDAMARRA CADD shares his inspiration for some of the powerful paintings that illustrate ***Listen*.**

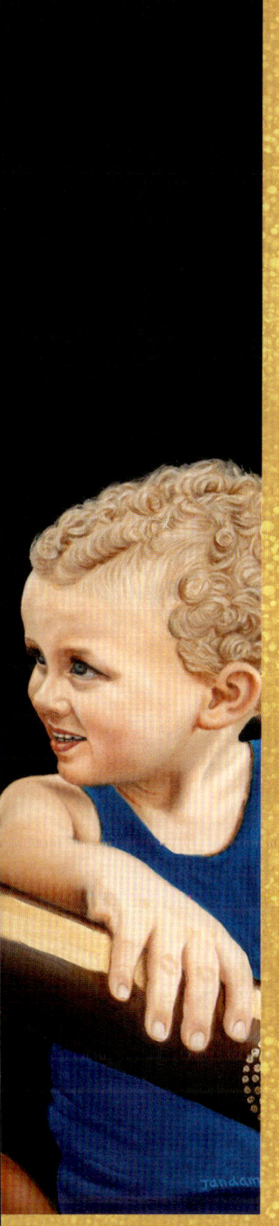

VIBRATION

As proud Kabi Kabi brother, Kerry Neil plays this ancient instrument, young Bowie is mesmerised by the vibration and the sound. I see this image as a beautifully symbolic representation of the younger generation connecting with something that is a part of the oldest living culture in the world.

WALKING WITH THE ANCESTORS

As Uncle Wiruungga Dunggiirr shares in ceremonial dance he is not alone. He walks in the footprints of thousands of generations alongside the Ancestors.

COUNTRY IS WITHIN

This painting is about showing the spiritual connection between ourselves and Country. Our connection to Country is integral to our sense of identity and wellness on every level. This painting celebrates Jacquie Sandy, proud Kabi Kabi woman, and her connection to Country, especially to the mighty Bunya tree.

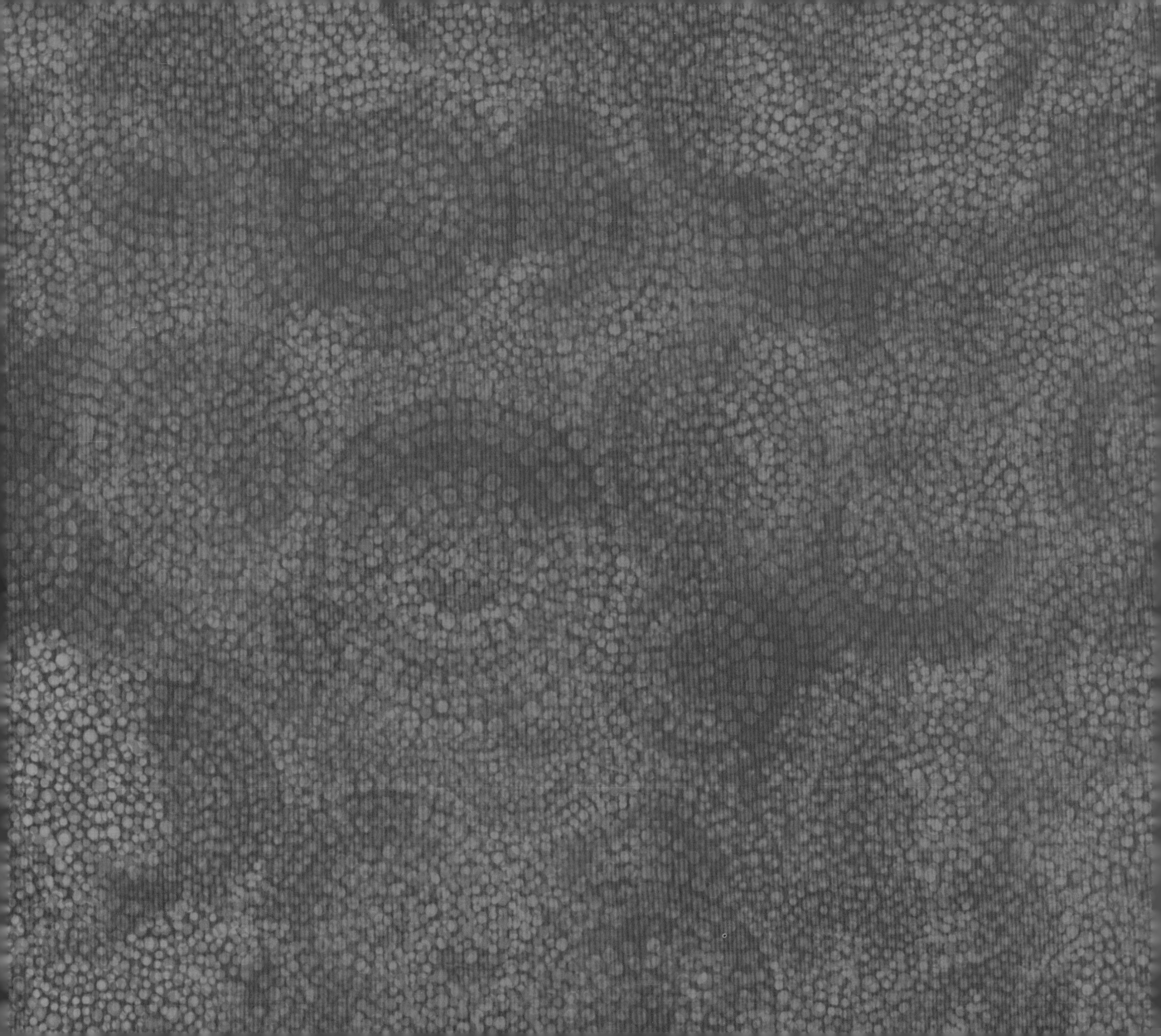